THE WEEPING LADY CONSPIRACY

A Marquess House Short Story

Alexandra Walsh

Table of Contents

THANK YOU!

A NOTE ABOUT SPOILERS

THE WEEPING LADY CONSPIRACY

THE HISTORY

ALSO BY ALEXANDRA WALSH

THANK YOU!

The Weeping Lady Conspiracy was written as a thank you and a Christmas present to all my readers for being so wonderful. It first appeared on my blog but I realised not everyone is on social media, so they might not know it even existed. This is the reason I am now releasing it as an eShort.

It is set after the events at the end of the trilogy but, after I'd written it, I realised, the action takes place slightly before the events of the Epilogue of *The Arbella Stuart Conspiracy* (something eagle-eyed readers will notice).

A NOTE ABOUT SPOILERS

For anyone who has not read The Marquess House Saga — *The Catherine Howard Conspiracy*; *The Elizabeth Tudor Conspiracy* and *The Arbella Stuart Conspiracy* — there are unavoidable spoilers in this story. I have done my best to minimise them but there are some which could not be avoided. Despite this, I hope you enjoy the story.

THE WEEPING LADY CONSPIRACY

Marquess House, December

Perdita Rivers stared around the Great Hall at the swags of greenery, the twinkling lights and the vast tree which she and her sister, Piper Davidson, had been decorating all afternoon. This would be their first Christmas at Marquess House since inheriting the estate from their grandmother, eminent historian, Mary Fitzroy. The previous year they had been in Andorra but this festive season, they would be able to celebrate in their own home.

"It looks wonderful," said Perdita as Piper climbed down the ladder from the scaffolding tower they had been using to trim the enormous fir tree and joined her. "You've done an amazing job."

"We did it together," she said, beaming at Perdita.

Yes, thought Perdita, as they wandered through the house admiring the rest of the decorations, *we did do it together, all of it, and we'll continue to work together; we're lucky to have the bond of being sisters.*

Piper glanced at her watch. "What time are we on parade?" she asked.

"6.30pm," replied Perdita. "Apparently, the fun is fast and furious!"

Piper laughed, tucking her arm through Perdita's as they wended their way upstairs to change. The previous month, Susan Mackensie had approached the twins asking if they would host a fundraising evening for local charities in the village of St Ishmaels in Pembrokeshire, on the Welsh coast, where they lived.

"Mary used to do it," Susan had explained, showing them photographs of previous Christmas events, causing a pang of regret to flutter through Perdita. "It's a short carol service in the chapel, with all the children dressed up, then drinks and mince pies in the Great Hall for the adults and a treasure hunt for the children."

Delighted by the idea of being able to continue a long-held tradition, the twins had agreed enthusiastically. With help from Kit Mackensie and Callum Black, Perdita and Piper had created the treasure hunt and, while they had been decorating the tree, Kit and Callum had been laying out the clues for the trail. Parting from Piper at the top of the stairs, Perdita wondered if Kit and Callum had finished the extensive trail around the house or whether she might be able to grab a quiet half an hour to examine the box of research Jenny Procter, the chief librarian and archivist, had given her that morning.

"As requested," Jenny had announced, giving her a cardboard storage box, "this is the transcript of the oldest personal item we have in the archive. It's a testimonial written by one of the nuns who used to live in the convent on Llyn Cel island and is dated February 1486."

"Thanks, Jen, it's great to have you back," Perdita had said.

"Is this for anything in particular?" Jenny had asked.

"I'm not sure yet," Perdita had replied, "it was more a whim to see how far back the archive went. Do you know if Gran ever worked on this?"

Jenny had opened the box and drawn out a folder containing a number of neatly typed papers. "She was aware of its existence because it's been translated and transcribed," she had said. "The original is in a mixture of

Mediaeval French, which was mostly spoken and written by high-status women, combined with a local Welsh dialect. It would have been quite a translation task. The transcript is detailed to a PhD student who worked with Mary for a while in the 1960s, a John Foster. He worked here for six months while he was writing his doctorate. From a quick look at the digitised version, there is no obvious marginalia written by Mary, but she may have read it and dismissed it — this period didn't fall into any of her preferred research areas."

Christmas events had overtaken Perdita and so she was yet to study the transcript, but now she was itching to read it.

As she entered her apartment, Perdita grinned. Christmas music was blaring, the fire crackled and the Christmas tree twinkled. From the bedroom, her fiancé, Kit Mackensie, was singing along to the festive tunes at the top of his voice, unaware of his unexpected audience. As he ended with an impressive crescendo, Perdita stuck her fingers in her mouth and gave a piercing whistle, before clapping wildly.

Kit poked his head around the door, his hair wet from the shower, a towel around his hips.

"How long have you been standing there?" he asked, suspiciously.

"A few minutes," she grinned. "I think we should consider a duet sometime!"

He raised his eyebrows as she walked towards the bedroom, all thoughts of a quiet moment to read vanishing. "I only sing in the shower," he replied, his eyes twinkling.

"What a coincidence," grinned Perdita, "so do I!"

Perdita loved Christmas carols. As an historian, she felt the palpable link, revelling in the words that had been sung in worship for centuries, connecting the singers of the present day with those of times past. On one side of her Kit sang, shooting her the occasional complicit grin, causing her to smother a giggle. On her other side, Piper allowed her ethereal soprano to climb to the rafters of the exquisite chapel in the Marquess House grounds, while Callum's melodious tenor seemed to ground it in Christmas magic. They were standing at the back, watching as the children from St Ishmaels processed up the aisle with lanterns, their parents, grandparents and friends beaming with pride.

There would be another service on Christmas Eve in the beautiful church of Monk Haven. The ancient building was situated on the edge of the village at the bottom of a steep valley beside a stream but, according to Susan, the service at Marquess House had always been seen as the start of the festive season.

"Mary loved Christmas," Susan had explained in an apologetic tone. "This party was her way of covering up the fact she missed you both so much."

There was no formal nativity play; instead the children read poems, many of which they had written themselves. Perdita listened intently, applauding loudly at the end of each recital. As they prepared for the final carol, 'Hark the Herald Angels Sing', she allowed her gaze to wander. The chapel was Kit's favourite part of Marquess House and Perdita could understand why; it was exquisite and reminded her of a miniature version of the Chapel Royal at Hampton Court Palace. For her, the vast library with its Tudor graffiti was the space she adored. As she thought about the past few years and all they had discovered, her eyes drifted across the walls, then came to rest on a wall plaque. Squinting through the gloom of the candlelight, she could make out the words: *St Adwenna, 1486.*

It was not something she had noticed before and she was intrigued. There had once been a convent on the island at the centre of their lake, Llyn Cel, until its dissolution in the 1540s and she wondered if this was connected to the long-lost order of nuns. Making a mental note to examine it further, she brought her attention back to the final verse of the carol, before being carried along on the merry crowd as it returned to the Great Hall and more festivities.

The wind howled and rain lashed the windows as Perdita, Piper, Kit, Callum and the rest of the Marquess House family hosted the excitable and, Perdita thought, as she topped up glasses, successful Christmas party. It was several hours later when they said goodbye to the final guest and collapsed into chairs in the Lady Isabel room. Suddenly, a crack of lightning lit the sky, its blue-white shimmer spilling through the slender gap in the heavy velvet curtains.

"I wonder if the Weeping Lady will walk tonight," said Susan, throwing another log on the fire.

"The who?" asked Piper.

"Our resident Christmas ghost," said Alistair in surprise. "Has no one told you the tale of the Weeping Lady?"

"Ghost?" laughed Perdita. "It's inevitable in a house this old but no, none of you have mentioned it."

"I assumed Sarah would have filled you in. She and your mother used to pester her father, Hector, to tell them increasingly gruesome tales," smiled Alistair, referring to the twins' godmother and best friend of their late mother.

"Our grandfather?" asked Piper, and Susan nodded.

Hector Woodville had died before the twins were born. They knew he had been a businessman but, having always focused on their grandmother, Mary, they knew very little about her husband.

"Your mother and Sarah created a book. Sarah wrote the tales and Louisa illustrated them," said Susan. "It's in the library, I think."

"Sarah's never mentioned any ghosts," said Perdita. "Do you know the stories?" she asked, turning to Kit, who grinned.

"Of course. Meg, Stu and I used to pester Mary and she would relate them with really quite terrifying embellishments."

He squeezed Perdita's hand when her eyes darkened with sadness. Another moment of family history which she and Piper should have been there to share. Perdita blinked, determined not to dwell on things she could not change. Glancing over at Piper, who was sitting with Callum and seemed similarly resolute, Perdita said to Kit, "As you're the expert, you'd better tell us the tale of The Weeping Lady," she said.

Grinning, he began.

"Long before Marquess House was built, even before the convent on the island was created, a tower stood on this site. It was a lonely place, windswept and desolate, looking out over the churning waters of the saltwater lake. Legend tells us that imprisoned within its bleak walls was a young woman, locked up by her cruel husband, who had married her for her royal connections and her fortune. He told the world she was mad and left her in the topmost room to die.

"It was said she could be heard scratching and pounding at the door, begging for release until all her fingers were broken and bloodied. On a fierce and stormy December night she died, alone and desperate. Her wicked husband sealed up the room and there she remained, forgotten. It's said on windswept, rainy nights during Advent, she can be heard weeping…"

"It all happens around here on stormy nights," interjected Piper.

"What do you mean?" asked Perdita.

"The Weeping Lady weeps, the Llyn Cel mermaid sings," she continued, referring to the legend of the mythical sea creature which they had been told about when they had inherited the house. "It's a veritable cacophony of supernatural beings…"

"You asked me to tell you the story," said Kit, and Piper held up her hands in apology.

"Anyway," he continued, "after her death, if there was a storm during Advent, the Weeping Lady could be heard sobbing in the tower and anyone who dared climb the staircase would see the grey figure of a woman pointing at the wall with a maimed hand, as she wept and begged for help."

For a moment, they were held spellbound by Kit's tale, then outside, another roll of thunder made them all jump.

"Creepy," said Perdita with a shudder, "and very sad. Imagine being imprisoned by someone who was supposed to love you." The idea made her feel queasy. Could something so awful really have happened in their beautiful home? "Have you ever heard her wailing?" she asked Kit.

"Once," he admitted.

"No way," spluttered Piper.

"When we were teenagers," he said. "Stuart and I dared each other to go up to the tower one Christmas Eve when there was a storm like this raging. We were nearly at the top when we both heard it: a woman sobbing. It was terrifying."

Perdita felt a shiver run down her spine. Returning to their apartment later, after bidding everyone goodnight, Kit went into the kitchen to make a drink, while Perdita threw another log on their fire. Pulling out the notes

Jenny had given her and taking a mug of hot chocolate from Kit, who had flicked on the television, she smiled at their cosy domestic scene and began to read, hoping it would banish the disturbing image of the woman in the tower left by Kit's ghost story.

The Convent of Llyn Cel Island, February 1486

From her position at the back of the stream of pilgrims, the Mother Superior, Sister Non, narrowed her eyes in disquiet. Hers was a small order of nuns, attached to the Knights Hospitallers a few miles away in the Slebech estuary. At this time of year, their tiny convent received few visitors, yet there was a growing column of excitable men, women and children, their voices eager in the frosty air, their breath rising in white clouds. Riding past on her chestnut mare, she caught snatches of their conversations.

"A miracle…" whispered a woman.

"The saint's body revealed after the storm last week…" a man murmured.

"Is it true, her body is perfect? Preserved by God himself…"

A sick feeling settled in the pit of Sister Non's stomach. When the invitation had arrived to attend her nephew's wedding, her instinct had been to refuse. She was nun; it was not her place to gad to family occasions, but as this had been a royal decree, even her bishop overseer had insisted she travel to London. In her absence, Sister Gwen, an ambitious and impulsive nun had been acting the role of Mother Superior, a position of responsibility Sister Non had given against her better judgement. It seemed in her absence, Sister Gwen had been busy, turning their quiet home into a place of pilgrimage.

A saint? she thought as she guided her horse through the throng. It was incomprehensible.

"Mother," called a voice, and she shielded her eyes against the winter sun to see their newest postulant nun, Sister Elen, waiting for her by the wooden gate that was the main entrance and exit into their grounds.

A slight girl, whose heavy blonde curls were resistant to even the tightest of wimples, Sister Elen shifted nervously from foot to foot. The youngest daughter of a local landowner, she had been promised to the convent as a child. However, Sister Non felt Sister Elen might not be suited to holy orders. It was often the case when children were placed in convents by parents who had never questioned the true desire of their offspring. Elen was happiest when tending to the horses the nuns kept and as Sister Non approached, Elen reached out, taking the reins to lead her through the crowd of watching pilgrims.

Waiting until they were in the stables — which Sister Non noticed were spotless under Elen's care — and out of earshot of the visitors, the Mother Superior dismounted and asked, "What has happened in my absence?"

Her tone was calm but there was a hint of steel in her words and Elen winced.

"Sister Gwen will explain," replied Elen, deftly unbuckling the saddle and leading the tired horse to its stall where food and water waited. "She is in your office, Mother."

"Is she indeed?" replied Sister Non, the fatigue from her journey evaporating as her fury with Sister Gwen rose. "When you have finished attending to Mab," she said, patting the horse affectionately, "will you bring my bags in, please? It seems Sister Gwen and I have matters of importance to discuss."

As the girl dropped into a deep obeisance, Sister Non swept from the stables, a sickening feeling of apprehension creeping through her like a chill mist. Hurrying through the cloisters, she saw a snaking line of pilgrims waiting to enter their chapel. If she did not know better, she would think their convent had become a new stop on the St David's pilgrimage, but this was impossible. They had no shrine at which to worship. She corrected herself; when she had left for London there had been no shrine, however, something had happened during her absence.

In 1123, St David's Cathedral, which was 20 miles away from the convent, had been granted a privilege from Pope Callixtus II in Rome. It was declared that two pilgrimages to St David's were equal to one journey to Rome. From then, the landscape around the cathedral had become a sacred pilgrimage as the devout viewed the shrines to its eponymous saint and another Welsh saint, St Caradog. Other relics and the nearby chapels dedicated to St Justinian, St Non — the mother of St David — and

St Patrick made the route a popular destination. For reasons she could not yet understand, their small island convent seemed to have become another stopping place on this holy path.

Hurrying along the corridor, Sister Non marched into her office where to her irritation, Sister Gwen sat at her wide desk, writing with her favourite quill. The younger Sister, caught by surprise, had the decency to blush.

"Mother," she gasped, splattering ink across her letter, as well as onto her nose. Her always-pink cheeks glowed even more brightly in her embarrassment. Almost tripping over her robes in her haste to perform obeisance, Sister Gwen looked suitably discomforted as she muttered, "I did not expect you until this evening."

"Evidently," said Sister Non, her voice calm and neutral, belying her growing annoyance. "Rise, for goodness' sake, and clear away your clutter." Sister Non slid into her seat, waiting while Gwen gathered her belongings, shoving them into a canvas bag. "Sit," she said when at last Gwen had stopped flapping. "Explain?"

"Mother?"

"Don't be coy, Gwen. Why are all these people here and why are they muttering about a saint? What have you done?"

Sister Gwen's mouth compressed into a narrow line. "What have I done?" she trilled, her tone defensive. "It is what the Lord has chosen to do and it happened while you were away, which suggests he favours my tenure as Mother…"

"I am very aware you believe you would excel in my position," sighed Sister Non, "but there are many things you must learn before you will be granted a convent of your own, one of which is to control your cruel tongue. However, this is not a moment for discussing your weaknesses, this is the moment for you to explain what you claim is the Lord's mysterious work."

Sister Non could see the fury in Gwen's eyes but she was unmoved. The woman was a liar and a bully, hence the reason for her reluctance to leave her in a position of power.

"The tower, your grace," said Sister Gwen eventually, "the storms ripped away part of the wall."

Sister Non's hands, hidden in the folds of her scapular, balled into fists, her knuckles white as she focused her attention on keeping her face and body serene, quashing any suggestion of shock. "The tower is used for storage," she said. "Did the lower floors continue dry and secure?"

"Yes…"

"We have survived many storms on our island; perhaps the price of our salvation is the loss of a human edifice," she suggested. "We have two towers, the one on our beloved island and its twin, the centre of the old manor. The loss of one would have been no great sacrifice."

"If it had fallen, it could have destroyed the old manor."

"Nobody lives in the manor," said Mother Superior. "Since the new king has taken the throne, the family has abandoned this property."

Sister Gwen gave a derisive snort before saying, "When we sent Dewi, the builder's son, to secure the structure before it could topple, he found something unexpected."

"Sister Gwen, I expected better of you," snapped the Mother Superior. "You put a young man in danger for no reason."

"My dear, there was great work afoot," replied Sister Gwen. "I believed we were in the hands of God and a miracle was being bestowed upon us. Praise our sweet mother, Mary."

Mother Superior closed her eyes, not wishing Gwen to see the mounting panic she felt sure was written with stark clarity on her face.

"What did you discover?" she managed to utter, her voice constricted.

"Sister Dilwar and I ascended the stone staircase, followed by Sisters Tegla and Elen," said Sister Gwen. "We had always presumed the tower had three floors but the violent storms had ripped away the roof and part of the wall to reveal a sealed door leading to another storey."

"Another floor? Was there anything within this room?" The Mother Superior could not look at Sister Gwen, who could barely contain her excitement.

"A shrine," gasped Gwen, "with a body wrapped in a white shroud. At her feet was a plaster plaque engraved with the words: *St Adwenna, blessed be thy martyr.* Around this was etched strange symbols and creatures.

On the altar behind the sacred body of the saint lay an intricately sculpted golden box with similar adornments and above her, the ceiling was painted to the glory of the Lord."

Fumbling for her rosary, the Mother Superior turned her face away, biting back her tears. "You believed this to be the body of St Adwenna because there was a plaque on the wall?" she snapped.

"We presumed this was the case," replied Sister Gwen. "I gathered the sisters to keep vigil with the beloved body until Brother Caradoc could come from St David's to advise us. He also drew the conclusion that we were in the grip of a miracle."

Mother Superior resisted the urge to roll her eyes. Brother Caradoc worshipped money more than the Lord and would have been delighted to find a way to increase his revenue from the pilgrims. Adding a new saint to the current roster would no doubt swell the coffers of the diocese even further. "Where is this body now?"

"The saint lies in the chapel, where, in time, Brother Caradoc suggests we will rebury her with due reverence."

"What of the tower?" asked Mother Superior.

"Dewi and his father have secured and repaired the sacred shrine. We were awaiting your return before a decision was made about its future."

"I wish to see it, immediately."

Sister Non was already on her feet and near the door; surprised, Sister Gwen followed. Neither woman spoke as they hurried to the tower. Sext was approaching but Sister Non was determined to see the room, even if it meant missing the midday prayers. Torches guttered in sconces on the walls and as they traversed the stone steps, monstrous shadows followed in their wake. With each step, Sister Non felt fear rising like bile, until, at last, the door stood before her.

Taking a steadying breath, Sister Non entered the shadowy space. The marble table on which the body had lain remained in the centre of the room, the golden box at its head, while as described by Sister Gwen, the plaque was situated on the wall opposite. The ceiling was a riot of colour, featuring mythical beasts: unicorns, yales, mermaids and griffons, intermingled with figures from the tales of Camelot. Tears stung Sister Non's eyes as she gazed around.

"Is this not a miracle?" whispered Sister Gwen.

"Indeed, it is," replied Sister Non. "Please leave me to contemplate this unexpected development."

"But the Sext bell will soon be ringing…"

"This is a sacred space; my prayers will be heard with equal clarity from here."

Waiting until Sister Gwen's footsteps had retreated, Sister Non stared around the square room, imagining the bed that had once stood there, the stained glass window that had thrown jewel-like light into this exquisite space, and the laughter. But that had died long ago, she thought. Tears welled in her eyes and this time she did not fight to stop them; instead they flowed noiselessly down her cheeks.

"Oh, Ann, my dear sister," she whispered into the silence. "Through my own weakness, I have failed you. How can you ever forgive me?"

It was when the Mother Superior had composed herself and was preparing to leave that she noticed a few small bones on the marble table. Tiny fragments that had fallen from the wrappings. Blessing them, she looked around and noticed the golden box. Wrapping the bones in a length of linen torn from her own wimple, she placed them inside and stowed them in an indentation in the wall. The following day, she asked Dewi to plaster over it, leaving the remains in the safety of the reliquary.

Marquess House, December

The woman's voice swam through Perdita's dreams, a whisper, a story, imploring. Perdita struggled to wake, desperate to be free of this uneasy feeling, when suddenly a deafening boom shattered the night, followed by a crackle and a fierce blue-white light.

"What the…?" gasped Perdita.

Hail lashed the windows, the wind howled and the roar of the waves on Llyn Cel added to the wildness of the elements as the storm notched up another level. Her heart pounded as her senses tried to catch up with the unearthly noises. Beside her, Kit was halfway out of bed.

"I think we've been struck by lightning," he said, dragging on his jeans.

A moment later, Perdita was pulling on her own clothes, winding her long dark hair into a messy bun as they forced their feet into boots and grabbed coats and torches on their way out of their apartment.

"The lightning rod should have taken the brunt of the blast," said Perdita.

As they hurried along the corridor, Piper called, "Perds, did you hear that noise?"

Piper appeared from her own apartment, zipping up her jacket. Behind her, Callum was tying his shoes.

"We think it's the tower," said Perdita as they ran down the stairs towards the oldest part of Marquess House.

The majority of the house was Tudor with a timbered central structure and winding red brick chimneys reaching endlessly towards the sky but at its heart was an old square castle tower from which the rest of the house flowed. This was where they were heading. It was the highest point and held the lightning rod. As they approached the arched doorway leading to the steep, narrow staircase, they ran past a vast window. Through the gloom, Perdita could hear the waves of their lake, Llyn Cel, shrieking and roaring.

"Do you think the Llyn Cel mermaid will walk tonight?" said Perdita, as she and Piper began to climb the narrow stone staircase to the top of the tower.

"It isn't the mermaid we need to worry about," came Kit's voice from behind them as they pounded upwards. "This is the Weeping Lady's tower and we're in Advent, which is when she appears."

A light flashed above them and Perdita paused, squinting up. "Hello?" she called, irritated with herself for the sudden tremulous edge in her voice.

"Perdita?" came the deep Welsh tones of Billy Eve. "There's a bit of a problem with the tower. The lightning rod took the bulk of the hit but the wind has caused havoc."

Billy and his brother, Larry, were the sons of Sarah and Alan Eve. Sarah was the twins' godmother and housekeeper at Marquess House; her husband Alan was head of security, as well as overseeing the grounds. Recently, Billy and Larry had joined the family firm. Larry now liaised with Perdita and Alistair about the security of the house, while Billy was helping his father with the maintenance of the land, house and the many buildings that made up the vast Marquess House estate.

"What's happened?" asked Piper.

"We've lost some roof tiles and there's flooding in the attic rooms."

"Is there much damage?" added Perdita.

"Enough," he replied. "I've called Geraint and he's suggested we secure it with tarpaulin until he can see it tomorrow. Larry's gone to fetch some and tools."

Geraint Williams was the architect Perdita and Piper had employed to help with the endless building and renovations that were required in such an old property. He was currently overseeing a number of their projects: the grotto they had discovered in the abandoned basements, the heritage centre and various other schemes.

"We'll help," said Piper, as they made their cautious way into the top room of the tower.

This was the oldest part of the building and the most fragile. The estate had always prided itself that it was one of the few ancient, intact castle towers in the area; now it seemed the vicious storm had other plans. On her first day at Marquess House, Perdita had considered taking over the tower as her own private space but the smaller rooms and the narrow windows, while ideal for a quirky few nights' stay, were not suited to modern home life.

"The thickness of the walls makes the wi-fi hit and miss in here," Kit had told her all that time ago as he had shown her the rooms which were used as guest bedrooms. "The showers are a bit feeble, too."

Now, as they stood in the attic space, Perdita stared around in dismay at the puddles of water sloshing on the floor, while rain continued to pour through the gaping hole in the roof. The original wooden struts lay smashed into matchwood.

"Oh, no!" she gasped, while Piper blinked at the damage through sad eyes.

"We'll be able to secure it," Billy assured them, "which will limit the damage, but this isn't all of it."

He led the way to the room directly below, where Perdita and Piper exchanged looks of misery. The water had trickled through the ceiling and down the walls, leaving a section of the ancient painted plasterwork, which Perdita thought might be early Tudor, hanging off the wall, dissolving and crumbling as the elements forced their way into the tower.

"Careful," warned Billy as Perdita and Piper picked their way towards the damage, while Kit and Callum hovered in the doorway.

"We need to secure it," said Piper, reaching towards the sagging mass. "Better to preserve it as a whole than let it fall on the floor and shatter. I might be able to restore it."

Looking around, Perdita pulled the woollen blanket from the bed and stripped off the top sheet.

"We can hold this underneath it to support it," she said, "then see if you can remove it and we can catch it."

She flung the blanket back across the bed, smoothing it out, so it was ready as a base for the fragile plasterwork.

"Are you sure?" asked Billy.

"If it falls, which could happen with the next gust of wind, we'll have no way of saving it," said Piper in a voice that broached no arguments. Glancing at Kit and Callum, she beckoned them over, then fixed Billy with a glare. "We could do with an extra pair of hands, Billy."

Muttering about Grade I listings, Billy joined them by the wall. Perdita took one side of the sheet, holding it like a cradle under the plaster. Kit was next to her and beside him Callum, while Billy took the slack on the other side. Using one of the smaller files from Billy's tool belt, Piper began to chip painstakingly away at the thin edge of plaster that continued to attach it to the wall.

"This is it," she said, raising her voice over the howl of the wind. "I'm going to tip it gently forward."

Holding her breath, Perdita tightened her grip, ready to take the strain. Piper tapped away the final piece and guided the chunk of painted wall onto the sheet. Together they carried it to the bed, where Perdita exhaled in relief. It was as they stepped away from the rescued plasterwork, she realised the room held another secret.

"Look," she gasped, hurrying to the wall where a secondary piece of plain plaster had fallen away, revealing a gap. It looked as though two bricks had been removed, and inside was a golden casket covered in carved symbols and letters.

"What is it?" asked Piper, a tremor in her voice.

Perdita itched to touch it but without protective gloves she was nervous of causing damage.

"It looks like a reliquary," she replied, the words of the nun's testimony running around her head. *Surely this can't be the same one?* she thought.

"A what?" asked Callum.

"They were repositories for relics, usually of saints," she replied.

"There are human bones in there?" asked Billy, sounding revolted.

"Perhaps," replied Perdita.

Heavy footsteps drew their attention as Larry arrived with his father, Alan, and Kit's father, Alistair. Placing the sheet over the plasterwork to protect it, Perdita reached into her pockets and pulled out a pair of leather gloves.

"Not ideal," she admitted, "but we need to put this somewhere safe." Easing the box from its hiding place, she laid it on the bed beside the frieze. "I'll call Mark in the morning," she said. "He can get the conservators up here and try to work out exactly what we've discovered."

As another thunderclap sounded, they all turned, eager to return to the attic space in the eaves to help Billy secure the tower and prevent any further damage. Perdita was the last to leave the room and as she pulled the door shut, a voice whispered, "Help me."

A chill ran through her but when she looked in the room and saw it was empty, she dismissed it as her imagination and the wildness of the storm.

The Convent of Llyn Cel Island, March 1486

"Ever since your house has become a new stop on the St David's pilgrimage," observed Brother Caradoc, running his finger down the columns in the large ledger, "the Lord has provided for this house in a most pleasing manner."

Sister Non forced a fleeting smile, trying to disguise the repugnance she felt for the obese monk. Sent from the diocese of St David's to audit their convent, Brother Caradoc had demanded vast meals four times a day, accompanied by the best wines. Even considering the amount of food he had consumed made her stomach churn, although, with the pains returning to her back and side, she could not entirely blame Brother Caradoc for her nausea. Its true root, she suspected, was in the poppy-based tincture brewed by Sister Elen. While it eased her aches, its strength made her feel woozy and sick. The pains had been increasing since the previous year and she was aware her time was short, which was why it was essential to end this nonsense about St Adwenna.

"However," she said, before Brother Caradoc could continue, "a missive has arrived from the Bishop of Cornwall, who states it is not possible for us to have the bones of St Adwenna."

"Why would he make such a claim?" Caradoc asked with a hint of pomposity.

"The church of Advent near Bodmin Moor in Cornwall has long since laid claim to the bones of St Adwenna," said Sister Non. "While St Adwenna might have been born in Wales, the daughter of Brychan, king of Brycheiniog in South Wales, the majority of her works are recorded in the Cornish parish of Advent."

Brother Caradoc considered her for a moment. "Perhaps the Cornish are mistaken," he suggested. "The bones Sister Gwen found were in a shrine with a carved plaque saying, *St Adwenna, blessed be thy martyr*, were they not? Why would these words be placed at her feet if these were not the bones of the saint? Equally, why was the body of a woman sealed in a room? She had been laid out with due reverence. It is my suggestion this was in order to preserve the sanctity of a blessed saint."

"Or, she is not a saint, perhaps instead a beloved wife or mother or sister who was greatly mourned?"

Brother Caradoc's tiny eyes flashed with spite. "Wouldn't you and your family be the authority on such a woman?" he spat. "Perhaps the reason you do not wish to praise the glory of the Lord and accept the saint is because you know her true identity."

Sister Non did not reply. The silence lengthened but she held Brother Caradoc's gaze. His eyes, almost swallowed by the folds of fat on his fleshy face, gleamed hard and unforgiving.

"It is a mystery," he said eventually.

"Advent has a prior claim on the bones of St Adwenna," persisted Sister Non.

"Are there any other saints you could adopt in preference to St Adwenna?" he asked. "A local Welsh saint of impeccable reputation? It would be a shame to lose the revenue your bones are creating for the diocese."

Mother Superior stared at him, aghast. "We can't choose another saint in order to suit the church," she exclaimed.

"The bones of St Adwenna have been discovered here," said Brother Caradoc with a finality which he emphasised by slamming the ledger. "It is not impossible that two saints may have shared the same name…"

"However, it is confusing," interrupted Sister Non, averting her eyes as the monk hauled himself to his feet, his enormous belly rippling under his cassock.

"Pray for guidance, Sister, and see which other name the Lord might suggest. Your own might be one to consider."

With great relief, Mother Superior watched the enormous monk board his carriage and trundle away into the gathering gloom of twilight. Returning to the chapel where Sister Tegla was replenishing the candles around the shrine, Mother Superior genuflected, before taking a seat facing the golden coffin where the shrouded body now resided. Sister Tegla gave obeisance, then scurried from the chapel, leaving her alone.

"What are we going to do?" whispered Mother Superior, gazing at the beautifully enshrined body. "Your husband left me instructions and I failed. Your resting place was so peaceful and your fear of the dark so great, it seemed kinder to leave you in the sanctuary you and Stephen created. In failing to follow his final wishes, I have let you both down and now I am paying for my weakness." Sister Non pulled her rosary from her pocket, running the amber beads through her fingers. "Even my rosary was once yours, a loving reminder of my younger sister," she sighed. "Forgive me, Ann, I didn't want you disturbed but perhaps the time has come to reveal the truth and ensure you are buried beside your beloved Stephen, at last."

Interrupted by the Vesper's bell, Mother Superior rose, ignoring the insistent ache in her side as she glided down the aisle to take her place for worship. As she tried to breathe through the twinges, her eyes focused on the plaster statue of Mary, the Virgin. To her frustration, the cross on her rosary unexpectedly snagged on her habit, causing her to stumble. Reaching out to save herself, she fell against the tomb of Sir Stephen Perrot. Unsteady on her feet from the combination of the throbbing pain and the lingering power of the poppy tincture, she crumpled into an undignified sprawl on the floor.

Muttering at the foolishness of her fall, she reached out to the tomb to help pull herself back to her feet. It was then she saw the woman. Her sight was blurred from her faint but she could make out a shimmering grey gown with jewels which suggested a lady of high status. As the woman raised her hand, Sister Non saw it was disfigured; two and half fingers were missing.

"Please help me," the woman said, her voice misty, distant.

"Of course, my dear," said Sister Non. "We have a hospital; you will be well cared for. Let me rise from this ridiculous position, then we can attend to your injury."

"Margaret, please…" the woman whispered.

"Ann…?"

Sister Non felt a wave of dizziness overwhelm her. She closed her eyes, trying to compose herself, unable to believe what she was seeing. Was it the poppy tincture or a true vision? By the time her nausea had passed and she was able to turn to face the woman, there was no one in sight. Confused, she called out as the nuns filed in for prayers. The last thing she saw before the sickening pain engulfed her was Sister Elen's terrified face.

Marquess House, December

Perdita sat in the library contemplating the book her mother, Louisa, and her godmother, Sarah, had created about the ghosts of Marquess House. From the description Alistair had given, she had assumed it would be exclusively about the Weeping Lady, but it was a compendium of tales, including a phantom cat, a serene nun and a young man playing a lute, all of whom supposedly drifted around the house at varying times of the year.

Fascinated by her mother's drawings and Sarah's lurid tales, she imagined the two girls poring over their masterpiece. The picture of the Weeping Lady was unexpectedly vivid, with intricate details of her maimed hand. It made Perdita shudder; the woman who had been drifting through her dreams, causing her disturbed nights had, the previous night, held up a hand which bore an uncanny resemblance to the one in the image. Pushing the thought from her mind, Perdita continued to browse the book of ghost stories.

Two weeks had passed since the tower had been struck by lightning. The storm had blown itself out by the following morning but its legacy was to reveal another unexpected piece of history. Overnight, in the room where they had discovered the plaque and the reliquary, a few pieces of damp plaster had fallen from the ceiling to show the corner of an ancient frieze.

When Mark Llewellyn, the head of The Dairy — the state-of-the-art, climate-controlled restoration department within the Marquess House research centre — had seen these faded images, he had ordered the site out of bounds to everyone but him, his team, Perdita and Piper. He had arranged for the decorated plaster and gold reliquary to be placed in Piper's care in her studio and had had a scaffold tower erected in order to examine the ceiling. An hour later, he had rung Perdita.

"There's a frieze on the ceiling!" he had almost shouted down the phone, such was his excitement. "It's incredible, you must see this! I think it's Arthurian;

there's definitely a Round Table and figures which I believe are King Arthur, Guinevere and Merlin."

All other projects had been put on hold as the work on the ceiling began. Meanwhile, Billy and Geraint had brought in their teams to mend the roof and make the space watertight again. Perdita was always fascinated watching the speed with which everyone at Marquess House worked together when there was an emergency. In the meantime, she had organised the research to discover the origins of these unexpected treasures.

Jenny Procter had delivered a small pile of documents the following day. "There's not much," she had said, "but what we do have is in remarkably good condition. I'm not sure even your grandmother looked at these. They didn't fall into any of her timeframes, rather like your nun's tale. You'll find that slots into this time period, too."

"This is a far better haul than I was expecting," Perdita had admitted, sorting through the papers before happily losing herself in this new quest.

However, after reading the new documents, the truth about the ceiling and the golden box remained elusive.

She hoped when a clue finally emerged, as she was confident it would, the tale it told would not corroborate the ghost story of imprisonment and fear. The idea of such brutality taking place in the tower continued to upset Perdita but instinct, as well as the emerging beauty of the room with its plaque and painted ceiling, told her this was not a room full of hatred; it was a place of love. No one would prepare such a delicate space for someone they despised, she thought.

The plaque was easier to locate in the records as it had been repaired when her grandmother had turned the tower into guest rooms. The notes Perdita had discovered suggested the plaque had been a Victorian reproduction but Piper's examination had dismissed this conclusion.

"It's much older," she had said, perusing the dating results of the plaster from their laboratory. "Probably fifteenth century, and now the debris of years has been cleared away, I've found a date scratched on the back: 1457. The patterns on the front match the ceiling and the scrollwork on the golden box. Although, why it's dedicated to St Adwenna is unclear."

"From what I've discovered, St Adwenna was born in South Wales but is best remembered for her work in the village of Advent in Cornwall," Perdita had said. "There isn't much on record about her but it seems she was often seen as the patron saint of sweethearts."

"Cute," smiled Piper, then her green eyes sparked with an idea. "Perhaps that's why."

"What do you mean?" asked Perdita.

"A saint celebrating sweethearts — perhaps the room was decorated for a much-loved wife," she suggested, "and that was why the saint they invoked was one connected with love and romance."

"It's possible," agreed Perdita, her heart lifting at this possibility. "The other thing I've discovered is that all the nuns at the Llyn Cel convent took their names from Welsh saints, but there was no Sister Adwenna, so you might be right."

There was one full working day left before the Marquess House research centre closed for Christmas, and Perdita was determined to read the last few pages of the ancient nun's testimony. However, in order to achieve this, she had hidden herself in the library, where she hoped to grab a few hours of peace. The next day would see what was the apparently legendary Marquess House Christmas Party, before everyone either left to stay with family or friends or threw themselves into the festivities in the house and surrounding villages.

Kit's siblings were also arriving: his elder sister, Meg, and her husband, Pablo; and his brother, Stuart, who was in the middle of the three. With them would be Callum's family: his mother, Dr Deborah Black, who ran the library in the Mackensies' home, Castle Jerusalem in Andorra, along with his brother, Elliot and sister-in-law, Sam, who were pilots. The party atmosphere was apparent in the research centre, and Perdita did not want to appear to be a killjoy by not joining in with the fun, but there was something nagging her, and she knew herself well enough to know she would not be able to relax until she had at least tried to resolve her growing hypothesis into a working theory.

Flicking open her laptop, she pulled up the digitised version of the transcript. This suggested the nuns once held, or thought they held, the bones of St Adwenna but the Mother Superior thought differently. However, it was the dates included in the nun's account which were causing Perdita the most curiosity.

If Sister Non had returned from a family marriage in February 1486, one referred to as a royal wedding, then, thought Perdita, this could only be referring to the union between Henry VII and Princess Elizabeth of York. The match had been arranged to unite the warring families of the Wars of the Roses and to seal Henry VII's claim to the throne after his victory at Bosworth.

Allowing her mind to relax and rove from place to place, she waited for connections to form between the many strands of information she had gleaned. As realisation began to emerge, a shiver of excitement ran through Perdita.

"Any luck?"

Perdita turned her slightly unfocused eyes towards Alistair Mackensie.

"Hello," she said, pulling herself from her reverie, "what can I do for you?"

"It's more what I can do for you," he replied, his blue eyes twinkling. "Kit will be over shortly but I thought I'd grab you for a moment before he monopolises you again."

Perdita laughed. "What is it?" she asked.

"Your grandmother was aware of the plaque in the chapel," he said, sitting beside Perdita and nodding towards a photograph of St Adwenna's carving.

"Really?"

"Yes," he said. "When Mary inherited the house on her 21st birthday, the restoration of the chapel was her first project."

"Did it need much work?"

"Extensive, although, to Mary's relief, a great deal of the original structure and decoration remained but it was hidden beneath panelling. Your ancestor, Lettice Lakeby, was no fool; she realised the ceiling bosses and decorations were probably original, so she decided to cover, rather than remove, them. The plaque you spotted during the carol service was hidden behind a cupboard for years."

Perdita smiled, trying to imagine her grandmother's relief when she discovered the ancient decorations. "Did Granny think there was a saint buried here?"

"I don't know," replied Alistair. "She had so many other things she wished to research, St Adwenna was forgotten during the ensuing years. However, I have uncovered something interesting."

"Which is?"

"The plans of the chapel," said Alistair, handing Perdita a cardboard tube. "These were filed separately from the other historical documents and I remembered them last night. Kit and I dug these out this morning. He'll be here in a moment; he's enlarging them so you'll be able to see the detail. I thought you'd like to begin studying the originals, though. They're a useful resource for knowing how many bodies are in each grave."

"Alistair, thank you," exclaimed Perdita, pulling the documents out and spreading them on the desk. "These are wonderful."

"As you can see," said Alistair, leaning forward, "there are several sets, the Victorian blueprints and building plans to box everything in, as well as a hand-sketched version of what was probably an original plan Lettice discovered in the archive, which is considerably older. The most interesting thing is the number of tombs marked on the early map, particularly as none of these tombs have survived. However, I do wonder if the bodies from these burials remain, as there seems to be a number of receipts for a stone-mason to carve place stones, which I believe may have replaced the old tombs. Now, I must return to my office and a telephone call with the Inland Revenue. Such excitements!"

Turning to the floorplan of the chapel, Perdita began to read the many names and noticed one which made her eyes widen in surprise: Sir Stephen Perrot, 1432–1471. Perdita was aware of the Perrot family but not dating this far back. Remembering a document she had read, she was rummaging through her notes, when Kit and Piper arrived.

"I recognise that look," Kit said, his voice a mixture of excitement and apprehension. "What have you found?"

"My hypothesis is still forming," she admitted, "but I could talk you through what I've got so far."

Kit sat opposite her, while Piper pulled out the chair beside Perdita. Arranging a series of photographs between her sister and fiancé, before pushing her hair out of her unusual grey-green eyes, Perdita began.

"When Mark examined the reliquary, he suggested it might have been a trinket box rather than a custom-made piece because the iconography was secular rather than religious."

"Yes, he told us it was gold, because there's no tarnishing," said Kit, "and from the style, he dated it to the early fifteenth century. The symbols were mythical beasts and what looked like a scene from the tales of Camelot, the King Arthur legend."

"Exactly, and as Mark's PhD is in religious reliquaries, he knows what he's talking about," added Piper, studying the images Perdita had selected.

"He also told me, apart from ours, there were only two other known convents in Wales in this period," added Kit, and Perdita jotted this in her notebook. "The one on Llyn Cel island was a small establishment and was linked to the Knights Hospitallers at Slebech."

Behind her, Perdita heard a whisper and a shiver ran down her spine. Forcing herself to ignore this, she placed a neatly typed transcript between them. "This is a deed of ownership for the land, then known as Llanismael," she said, twirling a strand of dark hair around her finger as she waited for them to examine the document.

"Llanismael," said Kit, "is this referring to St Ishmaels, the village?"

"Yes, but also our estate," said Perdita, glancing at Piper. "According to this, some of the land was given to the church and the rest, the portion around the existing 6th century tower, was given by royal charter to Sir Stephen Perrot on the incident of his marriage in 1457 to the Lady Ann Tudor, half-sister of King Henry VI, to build a house."

"What?" exclaimed Piper. "The tower that's at the heart of Marquess House? This is a royal charter for our house."

"I think so," Perdita said, excitement in her voice, "which means the tower is even older than we realised. However, that isn't the issue, it's the date of 1457. The Wars of the Roses began in 1455, so the date of 1457 is a touch problematic in that by then, the sovereignty of King Henry VI was in doubt. Not only that, there are no records of King Henry VI giving titles or charters to any royal half-sisters, only half-brothers."

"Half-brothers?" asked Piper.

"Henry VI had two known half-brothers," explained Perdita. "Edmund Tudor, 1st Earl of Richmond, father of Henry VII; and Edmund's younger brother, Jasper Tudor, Earl of Pembroke."

Kit stared at her in astonishment, but Piper said, "Explain more for the non-historians in the room, please."

Perdita smiled. "It begins with Queen Katherine de Valois," she said, "who was the wife of Henry V and mother of Henry VI."

"Henry V, as in Agincourt?" confirmed Piper and Perdita nodded.

"After Henry V died, Katherine married an attractive Welshman, Owen ap Tudor and had, depending on where you check, anything from two to six children with him. Edmund and Jasper are the best remembered, but there are various records suggesting Owen and Katherine had another son, Owen, who became a monk; a daughter called Margaret who became a nun and died young, as well as another daughter, Ann, although her existence is doubtful. There are few records of Lady Ann Tudor, and it's always been assumed she died at birth at the same time as her mother, Katherine de Valois."

"Oh Perds, no," groaned Piper, allowing her red hair to tumble forward and hide her face in mock despair. "What have you done? Have you found more missing Tudors?"

"Perhaps…"

"How did Katherine de Valois die?" Kit asked.

"There are two versions of her death; the first states that knowing she was ill, she retired to a convent where she died of an unspecified illness. However, other scholars suggest she died during or immediately after childbirth."

Perdita recognised the tell-tale glint of interest in Kit's eyes as he considered her words. "Couldn't both have happened?" he suggested.

"She retired to a convent in order to give birth and died either in childbirth or because of another unrelated illness?" asked Perdita, and he nodded. "It's not beyond the realms of possibility. However, what if the baby didn't die? This could be the mysterious Lady Ann."

"Which is great but what has it got to do with anything?" asked Piper. "I thought we were trying to find out more about the reliquary and the frieze in the room."

"We are, and I think it's all connected, not only to the Tudors but to the convent on Llyn Cel island too, St Adwenna and Sir Stephen Perrot."

The door creaked, making them all jump, and Callum walked in.

"Hi, gang," he said, "I come bearing news from Mark's team. His assistant, Pete, has got the results of the bones in the reliquary and they're human." Handing the report to Perdita, he continued, "Finger bones, and from the isotope testing, it seems the person was born in or around the Thames Estuary but spent most of their life in West Wales. They're quite small, so that would suggest female bones…"

"The Weeping Lady," said Kit, suddenly, and once more Perdita heard a ripple of noise behind her.

"The ghost?" asked Callum in surprise, then realisation flooded his face. "She has a maimed hand!"

Piper rolled her eyes.

"Do you think she might be buried in the walls?" asked Callum with all seriousness.

Kit stifled a laugh. "In the walls?"

"Why not? Her fingers were hidden in a cavity; perhaps the rest of her is up there, too?"

"She couldn't be," said Kit. "The walls are solid stone…"

"There might a bricked up alcove," suggested Callum, warming to his theme.

"There isn't," said Kit. "Dad told me that before Mary converted the tower into guest rooms in the 1970s, she had extensive work done on the walls to ensure they were safe, there were no cavities or bricked up alcoves. You've been watching too many horror films, mate."

Disappointed, Callum flopped down beside Piper, who squeezed his hand.

"I've been reading a testimony written by the Mother Superior, Sister Non, of Llyn Cel convent," continued Perdita. "There are a few pages left, and I wanted to check the original because the notes I have contain the comment: 'Extensive decorative marginalia'. I thought the patterns might give us a clue."

"Do you have it on your laptop?" asked Piper, and Perdita nodded.

"Fire it up, then," said Callum. "Let's solve this mystery."

Perdita and Kit exchanged an amused glance, then she did as requested. As the digitised pages appeared, all four of them gasped in surprise. Around the neatly inked words were the same images carved into the plaster plaque Piper was restoring in her studio and the delicately wrought designs on the reliquary. All of which echoed the images Mark and his restorers were revealing on the ceiling in the tower. Turning to the transcript, Perdita began to read aloud.

The Convent of Llyn Cel Island, April 1486

The candle guttered and Sister Non stirred. Sister Elen knelt beside the Mother Superior, a goblet in her hand, which she raised to the older woman's lips. It would not be long; the Last Rites had been administered, and Sister Non knew she was unlikely to witness another sunrise. The postulant, Sister Elen, had been her constant companion these last weeks and she had come to care for the child. Each day, her admiration for the girl with her innate gentleness, strength and courage had grown. It seemed Sister Elen would always do what she felt was the correct thing, even if this caused a sacrifice or loss to her own dreams. A lesson Sister Non felt many of the senior nuns were yet to learn.

"A sip or two will help ease the pain," Sister Elen whispered.

Sister Non reached out and squeezed the younger woman's warm hand with her bony one. "You are a sweet child," she said, her voice weak, rusty with illness. "Tell me, my dear, was it your choice to be a nun?" Sister Non knew the answer and she watched as the girl's eyes widened in surprise.

"No, my lady," she replied, her tone hesitant. "I wanted to marry Dewi but my parents insisted on my taking holy orders."

"Dewi, the builder's son?"

"Yes," Sister Elen replied, her eyes sad, "we've been in love since we were children."

A smile spread across Sister Non's face. "Now I understand why he is always here, finding work, in order to linger."

"Are you angry?"

"No, my dear, but I'm saddened that you are being forced to do something against your heart's desire," she coughed, her body shaking with the effort. "It is within my gift to free you from the cloister," she continued when she had recovered enough to speak, "should you so desire."

"You would do that for me?"

"Sweet child, I would do anything for you. In this most holy of orders, supposedly filled with women of piety and compassion, you are the only Sister who has cared for me as my life ebbs; the others are preoccupied with their saint." She waved her hand towards the elegant writing desk in the corner of her comfortably appointed cell. "Over there is a scroll. Bring it to me and I shall sign it. This will release you from the convent."

Sister Non waited for the postulant to rush to the table, to grab her freedom with both hands but Sister Elen remained in her seat, quivering with nerves.

"I will be able to leave, there will be no persecution, no threat of arrest?" she asked.

"You have not yet taken your vows," said Sister Non. "As Mother Superior, it is my decision whether you are suitable for this life. There will be no shame, no humiliation; this will be a gift of honour. I am also bequeathing you my mare, Mab, and, in the purse beside the scroll is a sum of money with which you will be able to build a new life. With luck, it will be with Dewi."

A moment later, Sister Elen placed the scroll and a quill before Mother Superior. Summoning what remained of her strength, Sister Non dipped the nib in the ink and with a few strokes, the postulant was free.

"I believe your name before you took holy orders was Brigid," whispered Mother Superior, slumping back against her pillow.

"Yes."

"Brigid, may I prevail upon you one last favour?"

"Of course."

"To take my final confession and set it upon paper. I know your penmanship is excellent; I have seen your work."

"It will be my honour, Mother," she whispered, reaching for the vellum on the table and positioning the inkwell. "But have you not given this confession to Brother Caradoc?"

"This is not my spiritual confession," she said. "It is the dying wish of an elder sister to a younger. Sister in the secular sense."

Brigid did not reply, her brow furrowed in confusion.

"Have the bones of St Adwenna been interred?" asked Sister Non.

"Tomorrow," replied Brigid.

"Fools," muttered Sister Non. "She is not a saint, although she was angelic and taken from us too young."

"You know who she is?" whispered Brigid, her eyes round with surprise.

"Yes, and this is what must be recorded," whispered Sister Non. "It is the body of my younger sister, Ann. She died in childbirth but, such was her fear of the dark, her husband created a tomb at the top of the tower where she could be bathed in light. This was the reason I chose the religious life in this convent, in order to guard my sister's body. However, I failed her. Her husband, Sir Stephen, requested that upon his death, Ann would be buried with him and their son in the double grave in the chapel. He told me that if he was with her, he could protect her from the darkness."

"What happened?"

"He died in 1471, due to his injuries at the battle of Barnet," sighed Sister Non. "His body was returned to us, but I didn't fulfil his wish. My sister was sleeping peacefully; it seemed cruel to disturb her. Now, it seems God has punished me for my weakness."

"It wasn't weakness, it was love," said Brigid.

"But where has my love got me? Ann will be buried in a single grave, under an incorrect name. Forever alone in the dark and with part of her missing," said Sister Non, remembering her orders to wall up the golden box containing the tiny bones. "She will haunt me and I deserve it. Sister Gwen will soon be Mother Superior, and she will not be thwarted in her desire to create her false shrine, but it is important the truth is recorded. Please, write down all I have told you and place it with my testimony." She pointed towards a canvas bag looped over the back of the chair where Brigid perched. "Perhaps one day, someone will be able to reunite Ann and Stephen."

A coughing fit rendered her speechless and exhausted. Reaching out for Brigid's hand, she whispered, "Do not let me die alone."

"I will stay until the end, Mother," Brigid assured her.

"My name," whispered the elderly nun, "return it to me before I die." She could see the confusion in Brigid's eyes. "My name is Margaret."

"God bless you, Lady Margaret," whispered Brigid, tears in her eyes as the Mother Superior's breath faltered, then stopped. Brigid crossed herself and gathered the scroll granting her freedom and the purse of money, before disappearing on the chestnut mare into the wild blackness of the Welsh night.

Marquess House, December

"I know where she's buried," said Piper as Perdita finished reading. "Those engravings are on one of my rubbings. It must be her grave; the coincidence would be too preposterous otherwise."

"Like brass rubbings?" asked Kit.

"It's for a project I'm working on," replied Piper. "Let me pop back to the studio and fetch my notes, then meet me in the chapel."

Perdita, Kit and Callum shuffled all the paperwork together. Perdita slid the floor plan Alistair had given her earlier into a protective wallet, then led the way through the house to the chapel. Piper arrived moments later, her A3 artist's pad under her arm.

"Up here," she said, hurrying to the back of the chapel near the font where she pointed to the wall. "There's the St Adwenna plaque and here's the grave marker where I discovered these." She flipped open her pad to reveal the original rubbing; opposite this she had drawn her own version, highlighting the details. Swirls of mythical creatures roamed around a woman, all matching the engravings from the plaque in the tower.

"Wow, Pipes, this is beautiful," said Perdita. Her sister smiled her thanks, then crouched down and using a powerful torch began to explain her discovery.

"Here and here," said Piper, pointing at the swirling patterns on the worn stone. "They're hard to see like this but the rubbing shows the intricacy. It wasn't until we saw the images on the testimony I made the connection."

Piper pulled up some images on her phone and passed it to Perdita. "These are from the plaque and the golden box. They're identical; there's no doubt they're connected."

"Do you suppose Sister Elen drew them?" asked Kit, standing up and returning to the floor plan of the chapel with the graves marked throughout.

"Possibly," said Perdita. "She wrote the confession for Lady Margaret. Maybe she even kept it safe until such time as she knew Sister Gwen wouldn't destroy it. From the other records Jenny gave me, it seemed Sister Gwen's tenure as Mother Superior was short. Six months later, she was replaced by Sister Tegla."

"What happened to Gwen?" asked Kit, and Perdita shrugged. "Did she die?"

"At a guess, it seems she might have been dismissed," replied Perdita. "There was a comment in the margin of Lady Margaret's testimony which must have been added by someone else later. It didn't make sense at first but I think it does now. The names of Sister Gwen and Brother

Caradoc were written together, but they'd been crossed through and underneath were the words 'In France, exiled'."

"They were exiled to France, together?" questioned Piper.

"Do you think they were in disgrace?" asked Kit, and Perdita nodded.

"Possibly for the creation of the false shrine, although I wondered whether they were having a fling too," said Perdita. "It seems the shrine of St Adwenna was removed from the pilgrims' trail around the same time and quietly forgotten. My suggestion would be that Sister Elen or Brigid, as she became again after she had left the convent, may well have delivered the truth to the new Mother Superior, and with the identity of the body confirmed as Lady Ann Perrot, rather than a saint, Sister Tegla sensibly allowed the matter to fade away. "

The others stared at her in surprise but from the back of the chapel she heard a contented chuckle which seemed to offer confirmation. Even though it was a friendly sound, the small hairs on the back of her neck tingled.

"But what I don't understand," said Piper, "is why the tale of the Weeping Lady is so sad. The version Kit told us was about a cruel husband and an abandoned wife."

"Legends grow over time," said Perdita. "Perhaps there were other tales about abandoned wives and forgotten loves that were reinterpreted as a ghost story."

They all exchanged a knowing look.

"I wonder if Brigid and Dewi got married?" mused Callum.

"Let's hope so," replied Piper. "Brigid had been through enough; she deserved some happiness."

Joining Kit by the floor plan, Perdita scanned it, trying to dismiss her unease. "Sir Stephen Perrot," she said, pointing to the map, then turning to the chapel, walking halfway down the aisle before pausing. "His tomb and its marble effigy would have been in that alcove." Sliding the pew away, she crouched down to inspect the engraved slab below. "Look," she gasped, and the others crowded around.

A huge piece of slate, aged and worn, stretched before them. The words *Sir Stephen Perrot, 1432–1471* were engraved in the centre, surrounded by images of unicorns, yales, mermaids and griffons, intermingled with figures from the tales of Camelot. Below this, Perdita could make out another inscription. "It says, 'Lady Ann Perrot, 1437–1457' and underneath, 'Her son, Charles, 1457'."

"But that doesn't make sense," said Callum. "If what the nun's testimony stated is true, then Ann was buried over there as Adwenna."

Kit smoothed the burial plan out on the pew, reading the tiny letters. "This says, 'Although the grave states that Sir Stephen was buried with his wife, Lady Ann, and their infant son, Charles, the survey of 1885 showed there was one adult (male) and one child in the grave'."

"How do they know it was male?" asked Callum.

"The height," Perdita suggested, "thickness of the bones."

"In which case, why does it say Lady Ann is there, and where is she if her bones are missing?" mused Kit.

"Probably because Sir Stephen commissioned the tomb, assuming his sister-in-law, Lady Margaret, who became Sister Non, would follow his wishes and he would spend eternity with Ann," said Piper.

Perdita wandered away, her mind buzzing with all the information they had gathered and in a moment of clarity, she understood, but there was one last thing she needed to check before she was able to reach back in time and help the two sisters who had loved each other as much as she and Piper.

"Kit," she called, and the others turned. She smiled, overwhelmed with love for the three people in front of her. "When you said that you and Stu heard the ghost, you were telling the truth? It wasn't Meg up there playing a trick?"

Kit shook his head. "She was away staying with a friend in St David's," he replied. "Why?"

"The Weeping Lady," said Perdita. "She's been haunting my dreams ever since the night of the storm, and I know why."

Piper gave her a curious look. "Where are you going with this, Perds?"

"I think the Weeping Lady is Lady Ann Perrot, or Tudor, as she was born. She was placed in the tower because she was so scared of the dark her husband couldn't bear to bury her unless he was there to protect her. Unfortunately, in an act of love, her elder sister Margaret decided to leave Ann in the tower and didn't move her when Sir Stephen died. Her body was reinterred by Sister Gwen under the name of St Adwenna, but they didn't bury all of her, did they?"

"What do you mean?" asked Kit but she could see the understanding growing in his eyes.

"Her fingers were left behind and interred in the so-called reliquary…"

"Which is why the ghost is supposed to point at the wall with her maimed hand," spluttered Callum. "She wants her fingers back so she's complete."

"Don't you think it would be the right thing to do to let Lady Ann finally lie in peace with her husband and son, her fingerbones restored?" Perdita turned to look at Piper. A smile was widening on her sister's face.

"Yes, Perds, you're right; it's time Lady Ann was allowed to rest and Lady Margaret's work was completed."

Perdita was never sure how Alistair organised things with such speed and efficiency, but as dusk began to absorb the grey tones of the stormy Christmas Eve, they processed into the chapel ready to move the bones of Lady Ann from one grave to another. After presiding over the carol service in the village, the vicar had agreed to this interment service. As the coffin was raised from the forgotten and incorrectly marked grave of St Adwenna and carried with dignity to the waiting tomb of Sir Stephen Perrot, Perdita, Piper, Kit and Callum, Alistair and Susan, Meg, Pablo and Stuart watched as Sir Stephen, Lady Ann and their infant son, Charles, were reunited in death.

Perdita felt a sense of relief wash over her as the ancient slate stone was replaced. As the others filed away, she, Piper, Kit and Callum lingered, their shadows flickering in the candlelight. Outside the wind howled, the waves of Llyn Cel crashed and rain lashed at the windows.

"Shall we go up to the tower?" suggested Perdita.

"To see if we can see the ghost?" asked Piper.

"To make sure we can't, so we know she's at peace," replied Perdita.

Running through the rain and back into Marquess House, Perdita led the way up the stairs to the mysterious room where this unexpected adventure had begun at the beginning of Advent. Opening the door, they crept inside. Perdita felt a shiver run down her spine, then Piper grabbed one arm, Kit the other and Callum swore under his breath. Standing before them were four shimmering figures, a man and two women, one of whom was carrying a smiling child. The man gave a deep bow while the two women dropped into obeisance before rising. The younger woman raised her hand, complete and elegant, then the image faded and vanished.

A wave of warmth washed over Perdita as she turned to look at the others. Kit was white-faced but calm, Piper was wiping away a tear and Callum was smiling.

"Well done, Perds," whispered Piper, hugging her sister tightly. She then slid her hand into Callum's and they disappeared back down the stairs.

Perdita paused, then felt Kit slide his arm around her. "You did a great thing here," he whispered, kissing her cheek.

"Thank you," she replied, a lump in her throat preventing her from saying more.

"Come on, let's go," he said, and as she allowed him to lead her from the room, she heard a voice whisper, "Merry Christmas", and a smile spread across her face as they hurried down the stairs to join the others and raise a toast to family, friends and love.

THE HISTORY

Once again, this is fiction, but I have drawn on real historical characters and events. The information about Katherine de Valois and Owen Tudor is correct, as are the details of their children. The date of the wedding of Henry VII and Elizabeth, Princess of York is also correct.

St Adwenna is a real saint and as discussed in the story, she was born in South Wales but is associated with the village of Advent near Bodmin in Cornwall.

Thank you to the real Deborah Black, who read and edited this story, and Gemma Turner for her marketing advice and general excitement. Thank you to all at Sapere Books.

Thank you to you too, for reading this story and I hope you enjoyed spending more time with Perdita, Piper, Kit, Callum and the residents of Marquess House.

The Weeping Lady Conspiracy
Dramatis Personae

Marquess House – Present Day

The Woodville Rivers Family

Dr Perdita Elizabeth Woodville Rivers – unexpected heiress to a vast fortune

Piper Eleanor Davidson nee Woodville Rivers – Perdita's twin sister, who inherits equally with Perdita

Mary Fitzroy – (deceased) Grandmother of Perdita and Piper.

(**Hector Woodville** – (deceased) Mary's husband. Father of Louisa.)

(**Louisa Woodville** – (deceased) Daughter of Mary Fitzroy. Mother of Perdita and Piper.)

(**James Rivers** – (deceased) Father of Perdita and Piper. Husband of Louisa.)

(**Cecily Fitzroy** – Mary's sister, mother of Randolph Connors.)

(**Lettice Hawkland** – ancestor of Perdita and Piper.)

Lady Pamela Johnson – Long lost family member.
Brad – Lady Pamela's husband.

The Mackensie Family

Dr Christopher 'Kit' Mackensie –Works for his family's company, Jerusalem. Lives at Marquess House. Perdita's fiancé.
Alistair Mackensie – Father of Kit, Stuart and Megan. Husband of Susan. Owner of Jerusalem and integral to the running of Marquess House.
Susan Mackensie – Mother of Kit, Stuart and Megan. Wife of Alistair. Integral to the running of Marquess House
Stuart Mackensie – Middle Mackensie child. Works for Jerusalem. Lives in New York.
Megan De León – Eldest Mackensie child. Runs Jerusalem from the family home in Andorra.
Pablo De León – Megan's husband. Works for the Andorran government.

The Black Family

Callum Black – Piper's fiancé. Younger son of Deborah Black.

Dr Deborah Black – Mother of Elliot and Callum. Chief Librarian and Archivist at Castle Jerusalem.

Elliot Black – Eldest son of Deborah Black. Pilot of the Jerusalem planes.

Samantha Carver (Sam) – Wife of Elliot Black. Pilot of the Jerusalem planes.

The Marquess House Team

Jenny Procter – Chief Librarian and Archivist at Marquess House. Distant cousin of Alistair.

John Foster – a PhD student who worked at the research centre with Mary in the 1960s

Geraint Williams - architect

Sarah Eve – Head of Catering and Events at Marquess House. Godmother of Perdita and Piper.

Alan Eve – Sarah's husband. Former Head of Security, now semi-retired.

Billy Eve – Eldest son of Sarah and Alan. In charge of building maintenance and architecture at Marquess House.

Larry Eve – Younger son of Sarah and Alan. Head of Security, referring to his father while he learns the job.

Mark Llewellyn – Head of The Diary. Formerly engaged to Izabel Barnes. Elder brother of Briony.

Pete – one of Mark Llewellyn's assistants

Briony Llewellyn – runs the Louisa Woodville Trust, the animal sanctuary based at Home Farm, the childhood home of Perdita and Piper.

Vicar – from Monk Haven church

Dramatis Personae
The Llyn Cel Convent

St Adwenna – body of the saint found shrine at the top of the tower in Marquess House. St Adwenna was born in South Wales, the daughter of Brychan, king of Brycheiniog in South Wales. She is best remembered for her work in the village of Advent in Cornwall and is known as the patron saint of sweethearts.

The Weeping Lady – an unhappy ghost who haunts the Marquess House tower during Advent.

Sister Non/Margaret – Mother Superior of the Llyn Cel Convent

Sister Gwen – an ambitious nun, standing in as Mother Superior while Sister Non is called to London to attend a family wedding

Sister Elen/Brigid – postulant nun, keen horsewoman

Sister Dilwar – one of the nuns of the Llyn Cel Convent

Sister Tegla – one of the nuns of the Llyn Cel Convent

Brother Caradoc – an advisor from St David's Cathedral

Bishop of Cornwall – angry at having one of his saints appropriated

Pope Callixtus II – granted a privilege to St David's Cathedral in Pembrokeshire in 1123. Two pilgrimages to St David's Cathedral were the equivalent of one to Rome

Dewi Evans – the builder's son

Rhodri Evans – Dewi's father

Local Saints

St David

St Caradog

St Justinian

St Non — the mother of St David
St Patrick

The Tudors

Queen Katherine de Valois – queen of England. Wife of first, Henry V. Second – Owen Tudor Mother of Henry VI, Edmund Tudor, 1st Earl of Richmond and Jasper Tudor, Earl of Pembroke.

Henry V

Owen ap Tudor – husband of Katherine de Valois

Henry VI

Henry VII

Edmund Tudor, 1st Earl of Richmond – husband of Lady Margaret Beaufort. Father of Henry VII. Half-brother of Henry VI

Jasper Tudor, Earl of Pembroke

Princess Elizabeth of York

Owen Tudor – a monk

Margaret Tudor – a nun

Lady Ann Tudor – half-sister of Henry VI. Wife of Sir Stephen Perrot. Mother of Charles.

Sir Stephen Perrot – nobleman who fought in the Wars of the Roses

Charles Perrot – infant son of Lady Ann and Sir Stephen Perrot

ALSO BY ALEXANDRA WALSH

The Marquess House Series (published by Sapere Books):

The Catherine Howard Conspiracy (The Marquess House Series, Book One)

The Elizabeth Tudor Conspiracy (The Marquess House Series, Book Two)

The Arbella Stuart Conspiracy (The Marquess House Series, Book Three)

Coming soon:

The Marquess House Saga, Book Four

Copyright © Alexandra Walsh, 2021

Alexandra Walsh has asserted her right to be identified as the author of this work.

All rights reserved.

No part of this publication may be reproduced, stored in any retrieval system, or transmitted, in any form, or by any means, electronic, mechanical, photocopying, recording, or otherwise, without the prior written permission of the publishers.

This book is a work of fiction. Names, characters, businesses, organisations, places and events, other than those clearly in the public domain, are either the product of the author's imagination, or are used fictitiously.

Any resemblances to actual persons, living or dead, events or locales are purely coincidental.

Published with permission of Sapere Books.

Printed in Great Britain
by Amazon

60645580R00047